Gordon's Porch

David R. Beshears

Literary Fiction
Adapted from the screenplay

Greybeard Publishing
Washington State

Greybeard Publishing
P.O. Box 480
McCleary, WA 98557-0480

ISBN 978-1-947231-58-0

Gordon's Porch

Chapter One

Carol turned the car into the driveway and eased it to a stop. She shifted it into park and glanced across to her father. Gordon was sitting in the passenger seat staring straight ahead. Neither spoke. The conversation during the drive from the funeral hadn't gone well.

She turned off the engine and climbed out of the car. She looked out at the neighborhood, then to the house. Her father's home was modest, middle-class, the house and yard neat, clean, well-maintained, as was the neighborhood.

Carol was fifty-four years old, slim, attractive. She was dressed now in dark clothes, a thin black veil draped over her well-groomed hair. She started across the yard to the front steps, climbed the steps up onto the large, covered porch that spanned the width of the house, the porch enclosed by waist-high wood railing. Four chairs were lined up, separated by small tables.

She turned now and stood at the rail, watched her father start across the yard from the car. Gordon appeared healthy, unhindered by his eighty years. He was dressed now in a dark suit, wore a black funeral band on one arm. His frown never left his face as he calmly took the steps up on the porch. He stood at the door, reached into his pocket for his house keys.

Carol turned and stood beside her father, pulled the veil from her hair.

"Dad. Please."

"Thank you for the ride, Carol." Gordon unlocked the door.

"Dad." She watched him open the door. "How about a cup of coffee?"

"Sure. This morning's pot."

He went into the house, leaving Carol to follow after him. He crossed the living room and entered the modest kitchen: Refrigerator, stove and sink separated by small kitchen counters. A 5-gallon water bottle was on a stand next to one of the counters. A small, square table and two chairs were at the far end of the room.

Gordon took a cup down from the cupboard, set it beside his own old battered cup. He filled both from the half-empty carafe, placed both cups into the over-the-range microwave. He pushed a button, watched the microwave start, watched the coffee cups move slowly on the turntable within.

"Dad. I know you're fine." Carol leaned against the counter, folded her arms and looked down at the floor. "But like it or not, you are getting up there. Hell, I'm getting up there. And like it or not, an eighty-year-old man shouldn't be bouncing around a big, empty house all alone."

Gordon continued watching the microwave.

"It's not big, and it's not empty," he said. "And it's not a house, it's my home. It was your home, once upon a time. Your bedroom was down the hall, on the right."

There was moment then of uncomfortable silence. The microwave dinged and the light inside turned off. Gordon opened the door and took out Carol's cup, held it out to her. She looked down at the dark liquid within.

"When Mom was here you had each other," she said. "You looked after one another."

"I'll make do." Gordon took his own cup from the microwave and closed the door. He went over to the table and sat in one of the chairs. He took several cautious sips of his coffee, leaving Carol to try to keep the conversation going.

"And if something happens?" she asked. "Next week? Next month?"

Gordon said nothing, absently took another sip from his cup.

"Dad? When was the last time you did the laundry?"

"I'm not a child. Don't treat me like one."

"Dad, please." Carol set her coffee cup on the counter. "All I'm asking is that you come with me and we take a look at the place together. Absolutely no obligations. We just take a look at the place."

"I don't need to move into some old-folks home."

"It's an independent living center, Dad. They'll take care of the stuff you don't want to deal with, leave you to do what you like."

"What I like, Carol, is living right here, in my own home. I've got friends here."

They again grew silent. Carol again leaned back against the counter. Gordon took another swallow from his coffee, stared into the cup.

He set the cup down onto the table.

"It was a nice service," he managed to say.

It appeared the conversation was over.

"Yes, it was." Carol looked from her father to the front door beyond the living room. "All right. I should go."

Gordon stared down at the cup, as if trying to decide whether or not to take another swallow.

Carol pushed off from the counter.

"I'll call you later?"

"I'll be here."

Gordon lifted his cup, set it down again without drinking. He watched his daughter start across the living room.

James walked up the middle of the quiet street toward Gordon's. He was a tall, slender black man is mid-eighties, with salt-and-pepper hair cropped short. He dressed in a clean button-shirt and slacks, used a cane but didn't rely too much on it.

He stepped off the street as he neared Gordon's, stopped as he reached the lawn. He watched Gordon's daughter Carol come out of the house and step off the porch. She walked quickly to her car and climbed in.

James leaned over his cane and gave Carol a '*good day*'
bow of the head as the car passed by and continued down
the street.

He continued then across the yard to the porch steps.

Gordon stood at the sink rinsing out Carol's cup.

He heard the doorbell: 'ding-ding, ding-ding', this
followed by knock-knock, followed then by another 'ding-
ding'.

James...

Gordon gave an almost silent grunt, took Carol's just
washed cup and poured the last of the coffee from the carafe
into the cup. He placed the cup in the microwave, pushed
the button and watched the cup through the glass window.

James waited patiently, sitting in the farthest chair of the
row of chairs.

His chair.

His cane rested against the rail in front of him.

The front door opened and Gordon stepped outside,
carefully juggling two cups of coffee. He set one cup and then
the other on the side table next to James and sat in the next
chair in line.

His chair.

"James," he said.

"Gordon." James took one of the cups in hand. He took a
sip, then held the cup in his lap. "Ah, Gordon," he said with
a sigh, letting the morning seep in. "I don't know. The view?
The ambiance, maybe? Something. I've told you this before?"

About a hundred times before...

Gordon didn't answer.

James gave a low *hmph* sound.

"Better than mine, anyway," he said.

"You don't have a porch. You have a stoop." They sat
quietly for a few moments, taking in the neighborhood. "You
have a back deck."

"That I do," said James, with an easy nod.

"It's a nice deck."

"Bigger than your porch."

"Bigger than my house."

They saw then a figure coming up the street in their direction. It was Lloyd Weaver, an elderly man in his seventies. Ignoring the sidewalks, he walked down the center of road, a large wooden staff in hand.

Shuffling past, Lloyd lifted his staff once in silent greeting before continuing on. They waved back in silent response, watched him continue on his way.

James took a swallow of his coffee, grimaced slightly and stared down into the cup.

"Is Carol still after you to move into a senior center?" he asked then.

"She is," said Gordon.

James indicated their neighborhood with a casual nod of the head, a glance at Lloyd Weaver's receding figure.

"You're already living in one, without benefit of bingo night."

"I don't like bingo."

"Then you're all set."

"I told Carol as much," said Gordon. "I don't think she gets it."

"Give her time," James said, a hint of a sigh. "She's a smart woman. She'll come around."

They took a few long moments then to let the quiet do its thing, to let the pleasantness of the neighborhood reach them and draw them in.

"It was a nice sendoff for Jan," said James at last.

Gordon nodded in silent response.

James gave a nod of his own.

"She would have approved," he said.

"She was easy to please," said Gordon. "Carol organized most of it."

James finished his coffee, stared down at the empty cup, another slight grimace.

"This morning's," he managed, giving a side-glance to Gordon.

"Waste not," said Gordon.

"Mmm. You say so." James gave another look in the empty cup. "Still."

Annie Romero stepped out of her small, well-kept house, locked the door and walked across the small front lawn, casually using her cane. She was an elderly Hispanic woman in her late seventies, was slightly plump but carried the few extra pounds well.

She started up the center of street, ignoring the available sidewalks, as did most of the residents of the neighborhood. The majority of the homes to either side were older, well-cared for, with well-manicured lawns and bushes, mature trees.

She passed several more of the homes of the pleasant neighborhood. A small, twirling lawn sprinkler worked to water the front yard of one of the houses.

Gordon's house was up ahead and to her right.

She left the street and stepped up on the sidewalk, started across the yard. Gordon and James watched her from the porch. Gordon gave a wave; she waved her cane in answer.

"Annie," said Gordon as she reached the top step.

"Gordon." Annie sat in one of the two empty chairs, leaned her cane against the rail in front of her.

The lone, remaining chair sat empty as silent note to their absent friend.

James spoke up then from his place at the end of the row.

"How are you holding up, Annie?"

"Holding up just fine, James," she answered. A few moments and then, "It was a lovely service."

James and Gordon said nothing, silently acknowledging that it had been so.

"A pleasant morning," said Annie at last.

"It is," said Gordon.

The three of them took in the morning, the gentle breeze, the neighborhood.

Their neighborhood.

"She was the best of us," said Annie.

She was," said Gordon.

James attempted a comment then, his words stumbling.

"When she departed this world..." the words trailed off, fading.

After a moment, Annie managed to finish James' thought:

"An empty chair on the porch."

The three of them, on Gordon's porch, in their neighborhood.

Miss McCarthy's collie Rocky made its daily appearance then, casually working his way along the yards across the street, taking care of his morning business.

A faint smile from Gordon, another from Annie.

James gave a slight grunt.

"Right on time," he said.

Chapter Two

Late evening. The interior of the house was quiet, empty, shadowed in gray. Gordon moved slowly from room to room as he closed down the house for the night. He walked down the hall, passing the door to his small office, then the door to the guest room, which had previously been their daughter's bedroom.

He hesitated then as he came to the doorway of the master bedroom. He reached in and flipped the light switch, turning on the light.

He looked about the room, then at the bed.

He moved then the rest of the way into the room. He walked over to the bed, hesitated before turning about and slowly sitting on the edge of the bed.

Morning. Gordon sat at the kitchen table, dressed in pajamas and a heavy robe, eating cold cereal from a bowl. The radio played in the background, morning jazz on NPR.

Late morning. Gordon, dressed for the day, used a manual carpet sweeper to clean the living room rug. Finishing in the living room, he worked his way down the hall.

He found himself standing in his office, next to his desk chair, one hand on the back of the chair, the other clutching the sweeper handle.

He looked about his office.

It was a small room, hardly bigger than a walk-in closet. There were several book shelves, one small curtained window. A desktop computer and monitor sat atop the cluttered desk. The lights were off, with filtered sunlight streaming in through a gap in the curtains. A poster of Machu Pichu hung on the wall above the desk.

A large collection of framed photographs was displayed on another wall, depicting Gordon and Jan's vacation pics over the years. There was a picture of the two of them hiking a high mountain trail, another on a tour on Galapagos Island. There was the picture of the two of them on a steep path halfway up a cliff beside a waterfall, another showing Jan pictured amongst a group of penguins in Antarctica. There was a picture of the two of them working the sails on a sailboat in the South Pacific, another of the two of them amongst a group riding a string of donkeys in the Grand Canyon.

Gordon leaned the handle of the carpet sweeper against the desk and sat in the chair. He shifted about, looked solemnly at the dark computer monitor on the desk.

He leaned back then, stared off in the direction of the curtained window, drifting mote-filled light brushing across his face.

Gordon stood before the washing machine, taking clothes from a laundry basket and shoving them into the machine. He set the empty basket aside, leaned forward and studied the row of buttons and knobs.

"It can't be all that complicated," he grumbled.

He turned from the machine and picked up the container of laundry soap pods, held it up before him and silently read the instructions. He opened the container then and looked inside.

What the hell...

He took out a pod, looked at it, somewhat perplexed, carefully studied it.

He looked from the pod to the contents of the tub inside the open washing machine.

You gotta be kidding me...

Another look at the back of the container.

At length he tossed the pod into the washing machine.

He looked again at the instructions.

He finally took out another pod, hesitated, tossed it into the machine.

He closed the lid. He looked again at the buttons and knobs on the face of the machine, reached out and pushed the start button. He hesitated. He leaned close, listened to the sound of water going into the machine.

Finally satisfied, he started toward the door.

Reaching the door, he hesitated, stopped. He looked back at the machine. He moved back to the machine, leaned in and again listened to the water going into the machine.

He straightened, gave himself a congratulatory nod.

"Right. Right," he grumbled to himself. "Not so complicated."

He started again toward the door. He stopped again, looked back into the room a final time, stepped then into the hall and away from the laundry room.

Gordon and James were sitting in their chairs on the porch, keeping an eye on the neighborhood, as what appeared to be their primary responsibility. All was quiet, peaceful.

Gordon gave a thoughtful sigh.

"You know anything about those soap pods?" he asked.

"Sure."

"So, you use them, then?"

"Sure."

A few moments of quiet contemplation.

"How many do you put into a load?"

"One."

"Not two?"

James curled his brow. "Why would you use two?"

"I don't know," said Gordon. "They're awful small."

"They're concentrated," said James. "You add your own water."

"Your own water?"

"Of course, your own water. You turn on the machine, it fills up with water."

"And one pod's enough?"

"How dirty are your clothes?"

Gordon gave a quick, involuntary look at what he was wearing.

"Not very," he stated flatly.

"Then one's enough," James stated firmly.

Gordon gave an easy nod in response.

A moment later a vehicle slowly passed by; a rare event and so notable, and so they took notice.

The quiet returned then.

"I put in two," said Gordon.

"Yeah?" said James. He shrugged then. "Won't hurt nothin'."

Gordon gave another nod. He reached over and picked up one of the two glasses of iced tea that were on the side table between them. He took a drink, held the glass in his lap.

"The last I remember, soap came in boxes," he said. "Powder."

"Hmm. Me, I remember jugs back in the day," said James. "Boxes makes you way old, my friend."

They both thought on that. Gordon took another swallow from his iced tea.

"I think France invented soap," he said at last.

"You think so?"

"I don't know it for a fact," he said. "Maybe. Seems right, though. Doesn't it?"

"Hmm," answered James. "I read somewhere they invented perfume."

"Really."

"Don't know it for a fact."

"Right," said Gordon, a half-snicker.

James gave a side-glance to his friend, looked out again at the neighborhood.

"I think I read somewhere they invented pants," he stated matter-of-factly.

That led to a very long pause in the conversation.

"Okay," Gordon stated finally. "Now you're just making stuff up."

James gave a half-smile, his attention focused out at the neighborhood.

"Hey," he said with a shrug. "Google it."

A moment later they note Miss McCarthy's collie making its morning rounds along the yards across the street, one yard, one bush, one tree at a time.

"Rocky," said Gordon. "Right on time."

James gave a grunt.

"A bit late, I think."

Gordon gave a quiet grunt of his own.

"You think wrong."

Gordon pushed his as yet almost empty grocery cart down the aisle, tall shelves filled with boxes of cereal towering on either side. A quite short, rather elderly woman was up ahead of him, pushing her own cart slowly, slowly. She stopped, studied the items on the shelves.

Gordon brought his cart to a stop and patiently waited.

The old woman gripped the handle of her cart with one hand then and reached up toward the top shelf, attempting to bring down a box of rolled oats.

She could just about take hold of the box, her fingertips brushing at the cardboard.

Gordon stepped around his cart and approached the woman.

"Awfully high shelves, aren't they?" he asked. "Would you like me give you a hand?"

"If you like," said the woman, bringing her hand down. She stepped aside and Gordon moved up beside her.

A young store clerk appeared then and hurried quickly up the aisle.

"Here, folks," he called out. "Let me help you with that."

"I have it, thank you," said Gordon.

"If you're sure." The clerk stood directly beside Gordon, hands on hips. "You wouldn't want to bring all those boxes down on your head."

"I think I can handle it," said Gordon, giving the clerk a side-glance. He brought down the box of rolled oats and handed it to the old woman. "Here ya' go, ma'am."

"Thank you." She placed the box into her cart and shuffled around behind it. She gripped the handle with both hands and continued down the aisle.

The store clerk watched her a moment, then gave a nod to Gordon.

"I'm just trying to offer a hand, sir," he said. "It's what I'm here for."

"Maybe you should put the old-folks cereal down low with the kids' sugar cereal," said Gordon, with more than a hint of sarcasm. "You know, so we can get to it without harming ourselves."

He returned to his cart then and continued down the aisle.

He quickly finished his shopping and minutes later pushed his cart through the automatic doors and exited the grocery store, one shopping bag in the cart. He stopped a few yards from the storefront, looked out across the half-filled parking lot. A wave of anxiety brushed across his face as he searched for his car.

"Crap."

A moment later a young attendant stepped up beside him.

"Would you like some help, sir?"

Gordon looked side-glance at the young woman, frowned and looked out across the parking lot.

"Crap," he grumbled again.

The sprawling grounds of the senior facility were well-manicured lawns, bushes and small gazebos. In the heart of the grounds were half a dozen large, interconnected buildings, one of which was enclosed within high, cyclone fencing.

Debra, the facility supervisor, a tall, middle-aged woman in her forties, stepped out of one of the buildings, with Gordon's daughter Carol right behind her.

Debra paused long enough for Carol to move up beside her and they then followed a wide sidewalk across the grounds.

"As you can see, Carol," she began, "our residents participate in a wide variety of activities, each to their likes and capabilities."

Continuing down the walkway, they approached and passed an elderly gentleman in his eighties. He was dressed comfortably, stood tall with the benefit of a walker.

"Don," said Debra, acknowledging the man with a nod as they passed. She noted Carol looking back several times at the elderly resident.

They paused then, both looking about at the grounds, before Debra glanced briefly back at Don.

"Not in every case of course," she said, "but a number of our seniors fail to recognize their diminishing capacity."

"Well, I don't think he's there yet," said Carol. "But I do have concern about my dad living alone at his age."

"And that's what we're here for," said Debra, with a sympathetic smile. She held out her hand and they shook hands. "I so look forward to meeting your father. He sounds like an interesting man. I'm sure we'll be able to answer any questions he might have."

"Thank you, Debra. I'm sure you will."

They exchanged good-byes then and Debra turned and started back to the main building. Carol watched her, noting again Debra giving the elderly resident an acknowledging nod as she passed him.

The man nodded in answer, appearing to say something to the supervisor, then watched her disappear inside. He turned then and started along the sidewalk, approaching Carol.

Carol waited for him to reach her, waited for him to speak first.

"Debra is wrong, you know," said the man. Don's voice was strong and clear.

"Excuse me?"

"We usually know," he said. "What she said. Diminishing capacity. Scares the hell out of us."

"I'm so sorry," said Carol.

"Yeah. Me, too." The old gentleman looked about. He nodded in the direction of a nearby gazebo, to an elderly woman climbing the step and going inside, taking a seat. "But we're not completely gone. We're not children."

"No, of course not," said Carol, increasingly uncomfortable. "Of course not."

They both then looked in the direction of the nearest, long, low building, this the building enclosed within high, cyclone fencing.

An elderly woman was walking within the fence, slow and hunched over a walker.

"That's Brenda," said Don. "She tends to wander off."

Brenda came to an awkward stop. She stood unmoving for several long moments, hesitant. She shifted about then, shifted her walker into position. Only then did she gaze outward beyond the fence.

"How sad," said Carol, shifting from discomfort to despondent.

"Yes," said the man, continuing to watch Brenda. "The center does care for all stages. I'll give 'em that. So, whatever my own future, I know this will always be my home. It's a comfort, knowing that."

He gave Carol a weary smile. She attempted a smile in return. She looked about the grounds and buildings a final time.

"Yes," she managed then, speaking softly. "There is that."

Gordon turned his twenty-year-old sedan into the driveway, pulled up slowly and stopped the car a few yards from the open garage. He turned off the engine, opened the driver door. He climbed out and opened the back door, brought out the one grocery bag.

James and Annie, sitting in their chairs on the porch, watched Gordon walk across the lawn and to the porch steps. He didn't appear particularly happy, taking the steps up onto the porch.

"Ah," said James. "Shopping, I see."

"What was your first clue," grumbled Gordon, continuing to the front door.

"Gordon?" asked Annie. "Is everything alright?"

Gordon didn't answer, shifted his grocery bag and used his key to unlock the door.

James leaned forward in his chair.

"What's the matter, my friend?" he asked. "Did they run out of hemorrhoid cream?"

Gordon continued inside without answering.

Chapter Three

Still half asleep, Gordon rolled slowly onto his back, let the filtered morning sunlight streaming into the bedroom do its job, to bring him fully awake. He stared up at the ceiling for a long minute.

It took a few moments more for the realization that he was alone in the bed. He kept his eyes focused on the ceiling, through the mote-filled rays of morning sun streaming above him.

He rolled again onto his side and sat up on the edge of the bed, absently sought out and slid his feet into his waiting slippers. He sat there a few moments more, looked back behind him. The blanket and pillow on the opposite side of the bed were barely disturbed.

Thirty minutes later, Gordon sat at the small kitchen table, dressed and ready for the day. He absently spooned cereal from the bowl as the radio played in the background, the morning news on NPR.

Bob was in his early forties, just about the youngest adult resident in the neighborhood. Working out in his yard, he could hear Gordon's lawnmower next door. He liked Gordon, and had very much liked Gordon's wife Jan, God rest her soul. The elderly couple had been great neighbors for as long as Bob and his young family had lived in the neighborhood.

When the sound of the lawnmower sputtered to a stop, Bob walked over to the row of shrubs separating the two yards to make sure everything was alright.

The mower was parked in the middle of the half-mown lawn, and Gordon was walking over to his porch. The old man picked up a water bottle, let out a groan as he turned about and sat on the steps.

He looked a bit tuckered out.

Bob slipped between several of border bushes and went over to see how Gordon was doing.

"A warm day, hey Gordon?" he asked.

"Not too bad," said Gordon. He took a deep swallow water.

"A bit warm for my taste." Bob lost the smile he had been wearing. "It was a nice service."

Gordon took another swig of water, replaced the cap. He set the bottle on the step beside him and looked up at Bob.

"Thank you for attending. You and your family."

"We all liked Jan very much," said Bob. "She will be missed."

On the porch behind Gordon: four empty chairs, one of them belonging to Jan.

"That she will." Gordon shifted to stand. "Back to it, then."

"You know, Gordon," Bob started, looking out at the half-mown lawn. "My boy would be glad to take care of this for you. You know, one less thing for you to worry about."

"Thanks just the same, Bob. I can handle it." Gordon stepped away from the porch steps.

"Absolutely. Of course," said Bob. "But the offer's there, should you change your mind. Jason takes care of a few of the neighborhood yards. Very reasonable."

"He's quite the entrepreneur, then."

"Oh, yes. That would be Jason."

"A good boy," said Gordon. He took several steps across the lawn toward the mower. He stopped then, stared long and tiredly at the mower. He let out a brief, tired sigh.

He turned then and looked back to Bob. Another, somewhat longer sigh.

"Just how reasonable are we talking here?"

§

Gordon, James and Annie were each sitting in what had long ago unspokenly came to be their assigned chairs on the porch. A pitcher and three glasses of iced tea sat on the small tables between the chairs.

Gordon and his companions were looking out at the newly-mown lawn.

"Yeah, I finally gave in and let the neighbor boy mow it yesterday."

"He does fine work, Gordon," said James. A hint of a grin, then. "A sincere effort, anyway."

"Yeah. He missed some," said Gordon. "Over there by the flowerbed."

"It looks fine," said Annie.

"And saves you for more important things," said James.

"Maybe." Gordon shrugged. "Suppose so."

James took a drink from his iced tea.

"You gonna let him mow it regular, then?" he asked.

"Probably. I told him I'd let him know."

"He does my yard," said Annie. "Once a week, this time of year."

"Does he?"

"He takes care of more than a few in the neighborhood."

"That's what Bob said." Gordon looked to James, then. "Yours?"

"Nah. My grandson," said James. "You know that. He comes over regular."

"Right. Right. John's oldest."

"That's right."

They watched then as Miss McCarthy's collie made his daily rounds, working his way from yard to yard across the street.

Annie put on a frown, crinkled her brow.

"Miss McCarthy has been letting Rocky out a bit later the last few days," she said. "Have you noticed?"

"I have," said James. "I hope the old woman's alright."

"She stays cooped up in that house and almost never comes out," said Annie. She continued watching Rocky. "I'll drop in on my way home today."

"Probably not a bad idea," said James.

"Ya' know..." Gordon started. "I can't blame her really. Sometimes, now and then, I just want the outside world to leave me alone. Not, you know, forever. Just... for a while."

"Hey now, my friend," said James. "Don't you be playing all gloomy on us. You'll bring down the porch mood."

"Not forever," Gordon said, defensively. "Like I said."

"Gordon, Gordon..."

"Sorry."

"Hey, are you still on about your sad little grocery store adventure? We've all been there."

"No," quickly. Defensively yet again.

"Not me," said Annie.

"No, no, Annie. Not valid," said James. "You have your groceries delivered. And you don't drive anymore."

"Neither do you," said Gordon, jumping in.

"I could if I wanted to. Just not much call, these days. Family takes care of most things." James gave a mental shrug. "I let 'em. It gives 'em purpose."

"Right."

"Maybe you could let Carol step in, do a few things for you."

Gordon picked up his iced tea, took a drink.

"I don't need it. I'm doing all right."

"Uh, huh. And that 'wantin' the world to leave you alone' thing?"

"Not the same thing."

"Right."

Annie let out a growl.

"Why don't you two quit squabbling?" she said. "Porch mood."

Now James picked up his glass of iced tea. He held it to his lips, mumbled over the rim.

"I don't know what you're talking about."

Chapter Four

Annie stepped off the sidewalk and walked across her well-groomed yard to the front door of her small, middle-class home. Stepping inside, she placed her cane into the umbrella bin beside the front door and walked into the front room.

The room was small, with thick carpet, an over-stuffed couch and chair with throw covers. A lithograph print of the Kennedy brothers (JFK & RFK) was displayed on one wall. A painting of Jesus with Sacred Heart hung on another wall.

A number of framed family photographs were displayed on a narrow table beneath the Jesus painting.

She turned on a table lamp and sat in the chair, took a few moments to allow the soothing atmosphere of her home to warm her. She looked solemnly across the room then at the collection of family photos.

She leaned her head against the back of the chair and closed her eyes.

James stood on his back deck, took in the quiet day, hoping to absorb the soothing atmosphere of his back yard. The deck spanned the width of his house, stretched away into the yard, taking up a third of the yard. Most of the deck was open to the sky, with only one end under a high canopy.

A high, wooden fence enclosed the yard, a lawn with clusters of bushes, garden sculptures, a birdbath. Several bird feeders were hung on shepherd's hooks.

The door behind James opened and his son John stepped outside.

John was in his fifties, tall and slender. He was dressed well in casual shirt and pants.

He wore a look of concern, sensing his father's solemn mood.

"You all right, Dad?"

"John. I'm just fine." James continued looking out at his yard a few moments more, finally glanced back at the house, the door. He managed a tired smile. "You all getting ready to take off, then?"

"Just about. They're all heading out to the car." John was still concerned. "Are you sure everything's all right?"

James gave another thin smile in answer, grew ever more thoughtful.

"When was the last time we used this deck?" he asked.

"Oh boy, Dad. Been a while, that's for sure." He considered, struggled to recall. "Jan's birthday, I think."

"Right, right..."

They both thought back then at the memory.

"I'm very sorry about Jan," John said then after a long moment. "I know how close you all are."

"Yeah, well... I guess I've just gotten used to having them around. Never really thought about it. We just happened." James considered again, finally gave a tired nod. "You know, we should think about having a family barbeque. Someday soon."

"Sure, Dad. That'd be great. I'll talk to everyone, see what we can set up."

"Good, good," said James. "Soon." *You never know...*

"Sure." John looked back behind them, then, to the house, to the door. He looked back to his dad then and gave a nod back over his shoulder. "I really need to get going."

"Right," said James.

"You sure you're alright?"

"I'm just find, son. You go." James managed another smile, lifted a hand and laid it on his son's shoulder, gave the shoulder a gentle pat and nudge. He lowered his hand then and gazed out across the yard. "I'll be heading out myself in a few minutes."

"You sure?"

"Absolutely." He managed a solacing smile. "I'm just feeling a bit nostalgic is all. I have a lot of years to look back on."

"All right. Well..." John took a step back, hesitated, then nodded in the direction of the house. "I'm off then. I'll give you a call later."

"Sure, sure. You go."

"Right. I'm gone." John headed to the door, then went inside.

The day returned to its natural quiet, then. James was alone then, standing at the edge of the deck, looking out at his yard.

A bird flew into the yard, alighting on the bird bath.

James watched as the bird settled into the center, began flapping its wings, splashing.

Gordon and James watched from Gordon's porch as Annie worked her way down the street toward them. She appeared to be relying more on her cane than was her usual.

As she was still some distance up the street, they continued their current conversation.

"How goes this year's travel mag article?" asked James.

"Mostly outline, some notes," said Gordon, shrugging.

"Really? Don't you have a deadline coming up?"

"Still have plenty of time." Gordon considered, hesitated. "I don't know, James. I'm having a hard time getting into it. I'm not sure I can do this one."

"I get it. I get it," said James, sympathetically. "All these years, the two of you on your yearly adventures; this is the last one."

"I'm just not sure," said Gordon. "I find myself just sitting there staring at the screen."

"Think of this last one as a tribute to Jan," said James. "A swan song. And don't forget, you have all those fans out there, waiting for this year's story. Where did Gordon and Jan go this year? Do I want to go there, go where they went?"

They watched Annie as she worked her way from the street up onto the sidewalk, then across the lawn toward them.

"Good morning, Annie," said James.

Annie took the steps cautiously up onto the porch, rambled over toward her chair.

"Annie?" asked Gordon.

"Fine, fine. Just a bit of a hitch in my get-along today." She dropped into her chair with a sigh. "I'm fine."

"You watch yourself, girl," said James. "Don't you let that get-along of yours get away from you."

"I'll do that." Annie looked to change the subject. "I dropped in on Miss McCarthy yesterday."

"Yeah? How is she?" asked Gordon.

"She has me worried, to be honest. I don't think she's doing nearly as well as she's been letting on. Just to look at her, she seems to be fading away."

"I'm sorry to hear that. Anything we can do?"

"Her cupboards were almost bare. I ordered some groceries to have delivered. She pushed back on anything more than that."

"Miss McCarthy has always been a strong-willed woman," said James. "She's been alone half her life and likes it that way. Except for Rocky, of course. I don't know how she'll handle it if the dog goes first."

"We're not meant to be alone," said Gordon. "Humans are social creatures. Family is important, whether by blood or by comradeship."

"Absolutely," agreed Annie. Her mind went back then, several years. "You were all there for me... when I lost Manny."

"You and Manny were family since before Carol was born," said Gordon. "You were Carol's Godparents."

"You choose your friends," said James. "Family is pretty much handed to you, for good or for ill."

Gordon gave a *hmph* grunt and looked sideways at James.

"I don't see that you have all that much to complain about, James," he said. "Your kids do well enough by you. They always have."

"Ahhh," dismissively. "My family endured my presence, true enough; but once they were out on their own, it was always their mother they came to visit. Now she's gone, it's all about duty to the old man."

"From what I can see, in spite of you being the grumpy old fart that you are, they do what they can to help. They're there for you."

"Yeah, alright. I suppose that's so," James grumbled. He sighed, then. "Guess I'll take that as a positive."

All three fell into a few moments of silent introspection, each lost into their own thoughts.

"Hey," said Annie then, breaking the silence. "Whatever happens down the road we have each other."

"And you can't get more family than that," agreed Gordon.

James looked side-glance at the others, then focused his attention out at the neighborhood.

"We'll schedule the group hug for later."

Chapter Five

Gordon and James walked casually down the center of the street, the hollow echoes of their canes striking asphalt the only sound. Behind them was Annie's house, up ahead to their left Miss McCarthy's. Further yet, to the right, was Gordon's house.

"You never said," James said, breaking the silence. "What'd Carol think of the old-folks home. She checked it out, right?"

"She checked it out," said Gordon. "Hasn't said anything one way or the other. I'm fine with letting the matter drop."

"Okay, but... you'd think she'd say *something* about it. Anything. But silent on the subject? That could be good, or oh, it could be really bad."

"And just what is that supposed to mean?"

James managed a shrug as they walked.

"Maybe they're planning something."

"Ha-ha," said Gordon. "It is to laugh."

"Just sayin'," sighed James. "Might be time to put the old geezer out on the ice floe. It happens to all of us."

Gordon gave James a *shut-up* look, and they walked in silence for a few steps.

"It does remind me, though," Gordon said then, then hesitated.

"And?" James finally prompted.

"Not that," snarled Gordon. "Just something I've been thinking about lately."

James waited and Gordon considered his words.

"The grandkids are having kids of their own," said Gordon at last. "I never really saw that coming. Great-grandfather? Me? Crap."

James didn't respond, having silent thoughts of his own.

They stopped walking. They stood silent in the center of the street.

Gordon half-turned and looked at his friend.

"With each generation," he began again. "My story fades a little more, grows a little more distant, more remote. I mean, sure, I'm a part of Carol's story, as her father. Her kids, I'm their grandpa, so I'm less a part of their story. But their children? My great-grandchildren? I play a very small role in their story, if any."

"Oh man, my dear Gordon," said James, and they started walking again. "You, my friend, are seeing the world all ass-backwards. Look around you."

James indicated their surroundings.

"This is your story," he continued. "This neighborhood is the landscape of your story. The old man that sits up there on your porch right beside you? Your best friend? I am a major part of your story." James nodded his head back over his shoulder. "Annie, living several houses down the street from you in your neighborhood. And Carol, always there for you. We are all parts of your story."

James slowly shook his head from side to side.

"Not to be cold-hearted, my friend, but it isn't your story that fades with each generation, it is the roles of all those generations down the line that grow more distant from your story."

They neared Gordon's house, started drifting toward the sidewalk and Gordon's front yard.

"I don't think Carol liked the old-folks home," Gordon said quietly.

Gordon was up early, showered, dressed and ready for the day. Finishing a quick breakfast, he filled his coffee cup from the carafe and started from the kitchen. He went into his office, flipped the switch to turn on the ceiling light and worked his way over to the desk.

He sat in the desk chair, swiveled slowly about and faced the blank computer monitor. He hesitated then, waited, set his coffee cup safely to one side.

He reached for the computer then and turned it on, then turned on the monitor.

He waited. He picked up his cup of coffee, looked from the monitor to the curtained window.

The computer made a beeping noise. He hesitated yet again, finally set the cup to one side and shifted forward, readied himself to work.

The afternoon was warm. Gordon and James sat in their chairs, taking advantage of the shade and the slight breeze. Gordon took a drink from a glass of iced tea. He glanced in James' direction as he set the glass onto a side table.

"James?" he asked. "Are you alright? You look kind of peak-ed."

"I'm fine," James grumbled.

"You don't look fine. Kinda gray and pasty. And way too quiet to be normal."

"I didn't sleep so well, is all."

"Okay." Gordon wasn't totally convinced, but finally went with it. "You should try melatonin. Works for me when I have trouble sleeping."

James gave Gordon the '*drop it*' and expression in answer.

"Fine," said Gordon.

They both leaned back then, seemed to sigh in unison.

Moments later then...

"My toes fell asleep forty years ago and never woke up," said James. "I've had ringing in my ears since that damned concert we went to in 1974. I've had two spinal fusions and my back still hurts; and I haven't had sex in eight years."

"An unsettling image, that," said Gordon.

James *hmphed.*

Gordon sighed.

"I'm happy to put a Salonpas patch on your back, but as for that last, you're on your own."

They both slowly put on the same grin.

"Thanks for the offer," said James. "But I can put on the patch without your assistance."

"Good news. Offer retracted," said Gordon. After a few moments, then, "Have I told you that I can't hear the alert ding of the new microwave?"

"What?"

"No ding."

"Ah. No, Gordon. I can't say that the subject's come up."

"Yeah. I think I'm deaf to one pitch. No ding. I have to watch for the light inside to go off."

"Hmm."

"Weird."

"So sad," said James.

"Yeah."

There was a very long moment of silence. The sound then of a car coming up the street.

"So... no to sex, then," said James, putting on a faux serious expression, watching the car approach continue past.

Gordon picked up his glass of iced tea and took a drink. He slowly set the glass back on the side-table, turned it about, leaned back again in his chair and relaxed.

"That would be a definite no."

Startled out of his sleep, Gordon came hurriedly into the living room from the hallway, scrambling to put on his robe. The room was dark but for the flashing of emergency lights come through the curtained windows. He rushed across the room toward the front door, hurried outside and took the steps down from the porch to the yard.

His neighbor Bob was standing on the sidewalk, looking up the street in the direction of several emergency vehicles that were parked in front of one of the houses, lights flashing.

As Gordon continued across the yard, Bob's son Jason walked up to his dad from the direction of the emergency scene. Bob listened to his son, nodded then and sent his son to their house.

"What's going on, Bob?" asked Gordon, coming up beside the man, looking up the street. "What's happened?"

"Miss McCarthy," said Bob.

"Oh, geez. Is she...?"

"I don't think so," said Bob, shaking his head. "Jason said she was conscious when they put her in the ambulance."

Gordon tried and failed to make out what was happening up the street.

"Let's hope, then," he managed.

As they watched, the emergency lights atop the vehicles turned off one by one.

"It looks like they're getting ready to leave," said Bob.

They continued to watch, attempting to make sense of what was going on. Eventually, the ambulance began to move. It turned about, started forward and came towards them. It approached, continued on passed them.

"No flashing lights," said Bob.

Gordon gave a noncommittal nod, said nothing.

Bob stuffed his hands into his jacket pocket.

"I would say that is either very good news, or very bad news," he said.

Gordon gave another noncommittal nod, but wore a very concerned expression.

Chapter Six

A car pulled up to the curb in front of Gordon's house. The back door opened as the driver hurried around and held the door open. He helped Annie climb out of the back seat. She leaned on her cane as she stood.

Gordon came out of the house and stood on the porch, watched as Annie gave a sign of thanks to the driver. She walked across the yard toward the porch steps. Behind her, the driver hurried around his car and climbed back in and drove off.

Gordon stepped aside as Annie took the steps up onto the porch.

"How is she?" he asked.

"They want to keep her another day, but she's doing better."

"She'll be coming home soon, then," said Gordon. "That's good news."

"She'll need to have home nursing for a few days, maybe longer, but yes." She stood at the rail, rested her cane against the rail. She looked at Gordon, then out across the yard. "She listed me as her next of kin," she said.

"You can do that?"

"Well, she did it, so yeah," said Annie with a shrug. "It was the only way they could tell me how she was doing, and the only way I could get in to see her, to look in on her."

"Hadn't thought of that," said Gordon.

Annie started, hesitated, finally started again.

"Listen. I hope you don't mind..." she began. "I have no one else. I registered you and James as my next of kin. Ya' know... just in case."

"Of course, Annie. I'd be hurt otherwise."

"Thanks." A moment's pause, and then, "Don't expect it to come up anytime soon, but just in case." She reached over and took hold of her cane. She stepped away from the rail. "Well, I need to check in on Rocky. He's no doubt missing his mama."

"Wait up. I'll walk with you," said Gordon, turning to lock his front door.

Annie waited at the foot of the steps. Gordon locked up and followed after her, the two then started across the yard and into the street.

"Rocky really is a sweetheart," said Annie. "And he's lost without his mama."

"How sad," said Gordon.

They walked in silence for a short while. Far up ahead and to the right, Miss McCarthy's house.

"Have you ever thought about getting another dog yourself?" asked Gordon.

"Someday, maybe," said Annie. "I don't know. Missy passing away was awful painful. I don't know if I could go through that again."

"I know what you mean. They're like family. They give so much, and it hurts so much when they go."

They approached Miss McCarthy's house, started toward her yard.

"Maybe I'll get a parrot," said Annie. "Great conversationalist and they live like a hundred years. Bound to outlive me."

Gordon was at his desk in his office, staring at the glowing computer monitor. The screen was filled with document text.

He took a long breath, reached out then and dramatically held a finger above the Enter key. He hesitated.

He pressed the Enter key, sending the article on its way.

He sat back then, stared at the screen a long moment more. He looked then at the window. The curtain was pushed aside, revealing the outside world.

Chapter Seven

Early morning. The front door opened and Gordon stepped out onto the porch, coffee cup in hand. Only after taking a sip from his coffee did he notice Carol sitting in one of the chairs.

Looking to the driveway... yep. Carol's car.

He looked again to his daughter.

"Carol, you're out and about kinda early," he said then. He held up his cup. "Coffee?"

"I'm fine, thanks." She held up her travel mug.

Gordon stepped around Carol and dropped down into his chair. They sat quietly then, taking in the morning.

Carol noted then Gordon staring absently down at his cup.

"What about you, Dad?" she asked. "Are you alright?"

Gordon gave a nod, took another sip from his coffee. He looked to his daughter and gave her a half-smile.

"I finished the article," he said then.

"That's great. Right?"

"Sure," he said. "I suppose so."

"So then..." Realization, then. She nodded then, looked down at her travel mug. "That'll be the last article with you and Mom."

"Done and sent," Gordon mumbled.

"It's a good story, though, right? I know Mom loved that trip."

"We had a great time."

"So... yeah, this is kind of like saying good-bye to her a second time."

"I let the editors know this was the last one," he said. "They seemed sympathetic."

"Of course," said Carol. "What now?"

Gordon gave a smirk, a shoulder-shrug and side-glance.

"Maybe I'll try my hand at writing home improvement."

"Ah." Carol gave a broad grin. "Fiction, then."

"Hey... now that would be an interesting angle on DIY." He tapped his temple. "Either way, gotta keep the ol' gray matter workin'."

"Sure, Dad..."

Carol stared down at her travel mug, Gordon at his coffee cup.

"Speaking of which," he started again. "I'm not sure I want to bring this up, but curiosity's getting the better of me. Was the old-folks home all you thought it would be?"

"Senior center."

"Whatever."

Carol hesitated, took a swallow of coffee from her travel mug.

"It was quite clean," she said then. "A caring staff. And there are lots of activities. It was all good."

"A ringing endorsement, that."

"They offer all levels of care, all stages; as residents move through their different support requirements."

"Wow," said Gordon. "That sounds like it comes right out of a brochure."

"Pretty much, yeah. But the residents I talked to do like that they won't have to move to a new facility when their needs change."

"Sure," said Gordon. "No doubt."

Carol lifted her travel mug to take a drink, changed her mind. She stared out at the neighborhood.

So quiet. So peaceful. A refreshing morning breeze.

"I do get it, Dad," she said softly.

"Get what?"

"The neighborhood."

"We like it," said Gordon. "My friends and me."

"I know," Carol struggled with a faint smile. "I have good memories of my own, growing up on this street. I had mixed emotions moving away, heading off to college."

"It wasn't easy watching you go. You were a good kid."

"You were great parents."

A few moments' uncomfortable silence. Gordon took a final swallow from his coffee, set the cup on the side table.

"Where is this going, Carol?"

Carol took another swallow from her travel mug, set it in her lap, looked out again at the neighborhood.

"The kids are grown and gone now," she said.

"Yeah. That happens. I think we just talked on that a minute ago. You. College."

"Yeah. Right. Well, I've been thinking about moving. Lately. You know, out of that big, empty house. It really is too big for one person."

"An apartment?"

"No. I've been thinking..." contemplative then, "An arrangement, you and me. I could move back in here with you." She sensed her father's walls going up. "It was just a thought," she said quickly.

"I don't need to be taken care of, Carol."

"Oh, I get that. It wouldn't be like that. You would go on just like you have. I would just be here, should you need anything down the road. All on your call."

"And this arrangement you mentioned? I'm thinking there's a bit more than you just being here should I need you."

"Nothing ominous," she said. "The deal would be, I would step in only as you need me, as long as I am able. But, if we got to the point where the needs were beyond what I could give, maybe we hire some help; then, further down, as needs change, then we might think about an assisted living facility." She held up a hand. "And that may never come up."

"Uh, huh. Right." Still, considering. "A thought, as you say."

"I'm not talking about playing nursemaid, Dad. I wouldn't follow after you with a damp washcloth."

"I need my privacy."

"Absolutely. We both need our space. We can work that out."

"Uh, huh."

"And one more thing," said Carol. "I won't be your housekeeper, either. We divide up the chores."

"So... roomies, then."

"Exactly. We'd be roommates."

"Right." Gordon was considering the idea. "Worth thinking about, I guess."

"Exactly," said Carol. "Let's think on it, then."

They fell silent, each thinking on it.

Carol took a final swallow from her travel mug, held it again in her lap and stared at it.

Gordon looked out at the neighborhood for a long moment, then reached for his empty cup, held it in his lap.

"So..." he started then. "You know those laundry soap pods?

"What?"

"Soap pods. For the laundry."

"Um... of course." Bewildered. "Convenient."

"How many do you throw into a load?"

"One."

"Really." Gordon frowned. "So does James."

Chapter Eight

Gordon stepped out his front door and onto the porch, a pitcher of iced tea in hand. James was sitting in his chair, glanced up as Gordon set the pitcher on a side table beside three empty glasses, then nodded out at the neighborhood.

Annie was standing on the sidewalk, watching Lloyd walking up the center of the street, tall wooden staff in hand.

"Moses, leading his people out of Egypt," said James, exchanging an acknowledging wave with Lloyd as the man continued past.

Gordon stood near the top step, rested a hand on the post, spoke back over his shoulder to James.

"I had an odd back and forth with him yesterday," he said.

"How can any back and forth with Lloyd be anything but odd."

"True enough." Gordon continued watching Lloyd walk slowly up the street. "I was taking a walk," he said then. "It was nice out. It was after that bit of rain we had in the morning, and the air was fresh and clean. Really nice."

He looked back at James, then gave a nod in Lloyd's direction.

"I said as much to Lloyd," he continued. "But to Lloyd, the morning wasn't nice at all. To Lloyd, it was all damp and gray."

"Sounds like Lloyd," said James, shrugging.

"Yeah but, that made me think. Damp and gray. That's the way Lloyd sees the world. He views his life through this gloomy, negative lens. I don't think I've ever seen the man smile."

"Yeah? And?"

"And... that got me thinking. How often, now, am I seeing the world damp and gray. Too often, I think."

"Come on, Gordon," said James. "You're allowed. You just lost Jan."

"Sure, sure. I get that. I do. But I fear that all these years, all my life really, it has been Jan and her insanely positive outlook on life that kept me seeing life fresh and clean after a morning rain. And now that she's gone..."

"She was certainly the sunshine in our lives. No mistake."

Gordon continued looking out at the neighborhood. Lloyd had passed on by and Annie was starting across the yard toward the porch.

"Yeah," said Gordon, a solemn sigh, watched Annie take the steps.

"And yes. You can be quite the gloomy fellow at times. But do not fear, my friend." James reached for the pitcher of iced tea, readied to fill a glass. He gave a smile to Gordon, then Annie. "You have us."

Annie looked back in the direction that Lloyd had taken, the man now gone.

"That Lloyd is a bit of an odd character," she said, and continued on to her chair.

James took a drink from his glass of iced tea, looked up at Gordon.

"So. Gordon. Are you gonna let Carol move back in?"

Early evening. The sun was just setting.

Carol had parked at the head of the street, leaned now against the front of the car, arms folded. She was looking down the street into her father's neighborhood. James' house was just up on the right, Gordon's midway down the street on the left.

The neighborhood was a single street, consisting of a bit more than a dozen homes; seven houses on the left, six on the right. Traffic was almost nonexistent on this street, limited to those few residents who actually had cars, and most of those drove only rarely.

And there was no reason for anyone else to travel down this side street. It went nowhere.

And so, when residents of the neighborhood were out and about, enjoying the tranquility of their neighborhood, they tended to walk down the center of the street.

Yes, there were sidewalks running along both side of the street, but sidewalks were for sissies.

The street, the neighborhood, belongs to us...

Looking down the quiet street into her old neighborhood now, Carol couldn't help but smile.

Gordon and James walked down the center of the street, in the direction of Annie's, each casually using their canes. There was a bit of a chill in the air, Gordon wore a light sweater, James a light jacket.

"Breeze is cool on the face," said James.

"I think it feels nice," said Gordon. He put the hint of a smile. "Refreshing."

"Enjoy it while it lasts, my friend. The days are growing shorter. Fall will be here before you know it."

"And then Indian Summer," said Gordon. "Best time of the year."

Up ahead then on the right, Miss McCarthy's house. As they drew nearer, they could see Miss McCarthy's dog Rocky sitting at the front window, watching them through the glass.

James used his can to briefly point in the direction of the dog and they continued their gentle pace.

"I haven't seen Rocky making his rounds the last few days," he said. "I hope Miss McCarthy is letting him out."

"She's been letting him out earlier, what with her life schedule all out of whack."

James gave a final look in Rocky's direction as they walked past.

"It doesn't look as though the dog is all that happy with the change in routine."

They approached Annie's house, up ahead on the left. As they drew nearer, they could see Annie in her yard, on her hands and knees, working in one of her flowerbeds.

They stepped off the street and onto the lawn, walked across the yard and stopped when they were within comfortable talking distance.

"Annie," said James. "I thought the neighborhood boy was taking care of that."

"Jason mows the grass. The flowerbeds are my job."

"Same here," said Gordon, looking over at James. "Don't you do any of your own yardwork?"

"Not so much." James called out to Annie then, "So, we're inspecting the neighborhood, to be followed by iced tea and cake."

"Minus the cake," said Gordon.

"Exactly." James held up his cane to Annie. "So, brush the dirt off your hands and knees and grab your cane."

"Sorry, boys." Annie straightened, still on her knees, held up her gloved hands. "You'll have to get by without me this morning. I'll be another hour or two yet."

"Ah. So sad, so sad." James turned away. "Later then. We'll save you a cookie."

"Minus the cookie," said Gordon. He turned to follow James. "Good morning to you, Annie."

Annie had already returned to her flowerbed.

"Thank you, boys. Later."

Gordon and James moved out into the center of the street and started back. They walked in silence for a time, enjoying the morning.

"We don't do this often enough," said Gordon after a time, breaking that silence.

"What? Walk?" asked James. "I walk. My house to your house. Back."

"Daily constitutional, then. Walks through the neighborhood."

"Not too bad," said James, looking about them. "Till the weather says otherwise."

They walked then in silence until they neared Miss McCarthy's house. There was a car parked out front now that hadn't been there earlier.

"Must be Miss McCarthy's home care nurse," said Gordon.

"Hmm. That would be really weird, letting some stranger into your life like that. Intruding all into your privacy like that." James thought a moment on that. "Still, I suppose it beats the alternative."

"It beats every alternative."

"What, there's more than one?"

"Dozens," said Gordon. "Dozens and dozens."

James to another moment to consider.

"Yeah," he said, at last. "I suppose that's so."

They continued walking down the street. The morning was quiet, the sun starting to take the chill off the day.

"You know what I'll miss most?" asked Gordon. "When I pass away? This. Times like this. No pressures, nothing that has to be done right now. Just... being. Just taking in these quiet moments."

They took several more steps as James thought about that.

"That works if you've a lifetime of experiences to look back on," he said then. "Right? They don't have to necessarily be major accomplishments, though a few of those would be cool, too. But... experiences. Hell, you don't want to get to the end, look back and realize you don't have any."

"Then I guess I'm doing all right," said Gordon. "I've had my share."

"You can never have too many experiences," said James. "You gotta be greedy when it comes to experiences."

"That sounds good in theory. But it looks to me that you and I are both starting to look back at those past experiences a bit more than we are looking ahead."

Gordon's house was up ahead on the right. They moved from the center of the street and then into Gordon's yard.

"Well, that's just because you're not putting the *looking ahead* item on the daily agenda," said James.

Gordon moved to one side, waved a head for James to take the porch steps.

"Age before beauty," he said.

"You are so last week," said James, climbing the steps.

Gordon followed after his friend, walked over to the small table on which sat a pitcher of iced tea. He handed one of the glasses to James.

"Although, if you think about it," said James, sitting, "Looking back is a lot less exhausting than looking ahead."

"Deep," said Gordon. He sat in the chair beside his friend, settled back, took a swallow from his glass of iced tea. "A moment to enjoy the moment."

They took a moment, then another, to enjoy the moment.

James nodded then in the direction of Gordon's yard beyond the porch.

"Your flowerbeds need attention," he said.

Gordon glanced over at the nearest flowerbed, said nothing. They took another moment then to take in the moment.

Gordon noted then the wedding ring on James' finger. He looked down at his own hand, at his own wedding ring. He worked at the ring with his thumb; the ring that had been a part of him for most of his life.

"I really don't see a reason to take it off," he said, staring down at his hand.

"What's that?"

Gordon lifted his hand, again worked at the ring with his thumb.

"Ah, right." said James, looking then at his own ring. "I did consider it, some time after losing Sadie, but in the end, it seemed almost a betrayal to take it off. I knew she was gone; I know she's gone, but our marriage remains. For me, it will always be so."

Gordon closed the fingers of his left hand, lowered his hand.

"It's been..." Gordon looked over at James. "Sadie. Six years now?"

"Next month."

"Right." Gordon grew thoughtful. "A great lady."

"Hell yeah," James said softly.

"All the more, putting up with you all those years."

"Hell yeah," a whisper.

Gordon looked down at his clasped hand. He slowly opened the loose fist, looked at the wedding ring.

"Yeah," he said, closing his hand again.

Time to change the subject.

"I told you, right?" he asked. "I finished the travel article. Done and sent it off."

"You made the deadline, then?"

"Two days to spare," he said. "I let 'em know, this is the last one."

"I suppose tears were shed?"

"They cried like babies," said Gordon, managing a grin.

"No doubt. No doubt." James took a long drink from his iced tea, looked out at the neighborhood. "Wow. The last one."

"Yup."

"So. I'll be cancelling my magazine subscription, then."

Chapter Nine

As James walked up the street toward Gordon's, he saw the bottled water delivery truck parked in front of the house. Reaching the truck, he stepped around it, tapped the bumper with his cane, and stepped up onto the lawn.

The delivery person was up on the porch, swapping a full 5-gallon bottle for the empty jug that Gordon had placed next to the door.

Coming back down the steps with the empty, the man gave James a nod hello as he passed by, returning to his truck.

James took the steps up onto the porch, turned about and leaned on his cane as he watched the man slide the empty jug into a slot and walk around to the front of the truck.

Gordon came out of the house and leaned on the rail with both hands.

James gave a casual nod in the direction of the delivery truck.

"How many times I gotta tell ya', Gordon?" he asked. "The city cleaned up the water like a year ago."

"I know that. I use the faucet for most things."

"And so?"

"So, the bottled water is better for tea and coffee."

James gave a *hmph* grunt.

"So you say. We should do a blind taste test someday." James glanced over at the tables between the porch chairs, noted there was nothing on them.

"Is the coffee about ready?" he asked.

§

Carol stepped out of Miss McCarthy's house, closed the door behind her. Stepping off the porch, she glanced back at the front window.

Miss McCarthy's dog Rocky appeared at the window, sat up tall and looked intently at Carol. Carol gave the dog a smile and wave before continuing across the yard and out onto the street. She walked up the street then, enjoying the morning, taking in the neighborhood.

Yes, she did miss it.

Reaching her father's house, she stepped from the street and walked across the yard to the front steps. She sat on the top step, elbows on knees.

This was soon to be, once again, her neighborhood.

She heard the sound of the door behind her opening and closing. She slid to one side and Gordon sat down beside her.

For the moment, he said nothing.

"It's little changed," said Carol.

"Not much." Gordon hid a smile. "The trees are taller."

She ignored that last. "But it feels almost the same."

Gordon gave a nod, took a few moments to admire his world.

Moving on then...

"Miss McCarthy?"

"She says to say hey," said Carol, giving a positive nod in answer.

"Say hey back."

"I shall," she said. "Rocky says hey."

Father and daughter sat quietly then on the top step, the porch behind them, the four chairs.

"So... Saturday, then," said Gordon.

"Yep. Saturday."

"Good, good," he mumbled softly. "Your room's ready. Didn't take much. Was pretty much the way you left it."

"I know." Carol gave a warm smile. "Thanks, Dad."

"No problem.

Chapter Ten

James stood on the lawn and waited, watched Gordon come out of his house, lock his door and take the steps down from the porch.

"Good morning, Gordon. All set?"

"'morning," said Gordon, and the two started toward the street. "Nice day, eh?"

They started up the street in the direction of Annie's house, walked for several minutes in silence. James was lost in thought, as if mulling over a matter of some importance.

Finally then, just jump right in.

"Don't get me wrong, Gordon," he started. "I do enjoy our walks. I do. And our conversations on any number of subjects. Our time here. All of it. I do."

"As do I..." said Gordon, warily.

"It's just, well, I've been thinking. Our talk the other day. You know. Experiences. Life experiences."

"Okay..."

"I'm think we need to stretch some. You know, while we can."

"Stretch..." uncertain.

"Exactly."

"In what way?"

"Well..." said James, considering. Up ahead on the right, Miss McCarthy's house. "Something more than pondering why her dog is late making its rounds."

"Uh, huh..."

"Beyond wondering whether Lloyd has always been such a prig."

"He has."

"I just think we need to look at ways to expand our horizon."

"Sure," Gordon said cautiously.

As they drew nearer to Miss McCarthy's, they saw her front door close, a moment later the silhouette of a woman passing by the front window.

"It's good to see her out and about again," said James.

"Close call, that," said Gordon. "Too close."

"And it definitely makes one think," said James. "Especially at our age."

They neared Annie's house up on the left. Seeing her come out her front door, they waited for her in the middle of the street.

"I'm not looking to replace your vacations with Jan, Gordon," said James, returning to their earlier conversation. "I'm just thinking that as a group, we should think about adding a few more experiences, while we still can. Like we talked about."

Annie stepped up beside them.

"What are you two on about now?" she asked, as they started back up the street.

"Adventures for old people," said James.

"Ah. Rousing," said Annie. "What'd you have in mind?"

"I haven't got that far."

"A kind of a bucket list thing?"

"I wouldn't put it quite like that, but yeah, I suppose so."

"James is thinking we need to seek out experiences as a group," said Gordon. "Adventures beyond our neighborhood."

"An adventure now and then can only add to our lives here in our neighborhood," said James. "Add color."

Annie looked to Gordon.

"Like you and Jan did," she said.

"I never really thought about it like that," said Gordon, considering. "But yeah, I suppose our trips did make our lives here in the neighborhood all the better."

"Well then, count me in," said Annie. "I'll just need to check my calendar."

They continued past Miss McCarthy's house. Rocky was sitting at the window.

They walked in silence for another long while, the quiet of the neighborhood wrapping about them.

"So," said James. "Carol moves in on Saturday, then?"

The rays of the early morning sun splashed across the lawns and rooftops of the neighborhood, the damp asphalt of the street shimmering beneath the thin mist of evaporating dew.

Gordon came of the house just as Carol walked from her car, parked in the driveway. He took a sip from his coffee as he watched her climb the steps.

"Carol," he said. "You're two days early. To what do I owe this visit?"

"Can I just drop by to visit my Dad?"

"Doubtful, but okay." He held up his cup then. "Get you some coffee? Or maybe some hot tea? It'll only take a minute."

"I can get it," said Carol. "I know where the kitchen is."

She stepped past her father and went into the house.

Gordon moved to the top of the steps. He took a moment to think on the situation. He looked back over his shoulder at the open doorway. He looked forward again, his expression thoughtful, considered, a hint of suspicion.

In the house, in the kitchen, Carol reached up into the cupboard and brought down a coffee cup. Curious, she looked again into the cupboard. She reached in again, brought down another cup.

She studied the cup.

The cup had been made by a child. The writing baked into the side read: World's Best Mom.

She clutched tightly at the cup, near tears.

§

Back on the porch, Gordon began to wonder what was taking Carol so long. He glanced back at the doorway. He looked out at the neighborhood. He took a final swallow of his coffee, looked down at the empty cup.

He set the cup on the rail, looked out again at the neighborhood, back again at the doorway.

Carol was sitting on the edge of the twin bed in the guest room, clutching at the handmade cup.

The room was smaller than the master bedroom, but still large enough to feel roomy. It was fully furnished: a twin bed, dresser, student desk and chair, book shelves.

Gordon appeared in the doorway. He stood there a moment, watched Carol a few moments more, finally moved into the room.

"I wondered where you had gotten to," he said.

"Sorry."

Gordon moved in to stand beside the bed. He sat beside his daughter. He looked about them, looked about the room.

"We tried to think of this as the guest room, once you went off to college. But this was always Carol's room. Your room."

Carol managed a faint smile, said nothing.

Gordon shrugged.

"Eh. We were always a bit light on guests, anyway."

He looked down at the cup that Carol was clutching. A nostalgic expression brushed across his face.

"Quite a project, that," he said. "God, your mom loved that cup."

Carol looked down at the cup. Her smile was sad.

"I was terrified it was going to fall apart the first time she used it," she managed to say.

"You did a great job," said Gordon. "We were so proud."

The room fell quiet as both thought back to all those years ago.

"Don't put it in the microwave," Gordon said at last. "It gets really hot. Damn thing'll burn off your fingerprints."

"I remember," said Carol. She looked up from her cup, turned her head and looked away. She fought back tears. Slowly then, she fought back sobs.

Gordon reached out, placed an arm around his daughter. Feeling her sobs start, he held her close.

"I know," he said softly.

Carol managed several sharp nods. The sobs came uncontrolled then, deep sobs.

Gordon wrapped both arms fully about his daughter. He struggled to fight back tears of his own.

It wasn't long, the tears came then.

"Me too," said Gordon. More tears. "Me too..."

They sat there on the edge of the twin bed in Carol's old room for a long time, Carol clutching the cup, Gordon holding his daughter close.

Miss McCarthy's front door opened a crack and Rocky squeezed out through the opening. He scrambled down into the yard as the door closed behind him. He hurried about, sniffing at one bush and another before casually strolling to the side yard and disappearing from view.

The silhouette of a woman passed before the front window.

Gordon, James and Annie were sitting in their assigned chairs on Gordon's porch. A pitcher of iced tea waited on one of the tables, half-full glasses near to hand.

"My own fault really," said Gordon. "When I agreed to Carol moving in, I had completely forgotten about her dog. And don't think I haven't noticed that she didn't bring the matter up in our discussions."

"I think he's a wonderful dog, Gordon," said Annie. "And you know what they say about the benefits of having a pet."

"You want to see the downside, take a look at the back yard."

"What's he doing to the back yard?" asked James.

"Landmines," said Gordon. "Lots of landmines."

"Oh, now you're complaining just to complain," said Annie. "She said she'll pick up the poop."

"That is exactly what she said when she was eight and we brought Sheba home. Guess who ended up pulling poop pickup duty?"

"Carol's grown some since then."

James grunted. "Kids'll always be kids," he grumbled. "They can't help it. It's in their nature."

"James..." Annie chided.

"Still," James conceded, "he is a nice dog. And well-behaved, from what I can tell."

"I'll give you that," Gordon agreed, finally. "Marley is almost as good a dog as Sheba, God rest her soul."

The group fell silent then.

Miss McCarthy's dog Rocky appeared across the street, making his daily rounds from one yard to the next, taking care of business.

"You know," James said, watching the dog move to the next yard. "I don't think I've ever seen that dog poop. Pees at one bush and another, never poops. How is that possible?"

"He poops in his own yard before heading out," said Annie.

"Really?"

"Same place. The side yard. Miss McCarthy uses the hose on the pile every day."

"Really?" asked Gordon. He thought on that. "So that means that you..."

"Afraid so. When Miss McCarthy was down, it fell to me as her surrogate next of kin to jet spray Rocky's poop."

"I gotta say," Gordon said after considering, followed by a sly grin. "You are quite the friend, Annie."

"Not a chance, Gordon," said Annie, quite decisively. "Marley's poops are yours to deal with."

Carol came out of the house at that moment, stood tall, arms folded.

"Well, it's good to know that the intellectual standards of conversation here on the porch haven't waned over time."

Gordon glanced up at Carol, offered his daughter the empty chair, Jan's chair, with the casual wave of the hand.

"We're all about delving into the unknown, exploring the unexplored," he said.

"Right, right." Carol gave a knowing smile, took the offered chair, glanced outward. "That includes your plans for... it's tonight, right?"

"Not my idea," grumbled Gordon.

"Right," said Carol, nodding.

James, who was settled comfortably in his chair at the far end of the line of chairs, gave a smirk, a chuckle, said nothing as he kept his attention out on the neighborhood.

Annie spoke up a bit apologetically.

"It should be fun," she said.

"Oh, I agree," said Carol. "It's just, well, rather unexpected."

"Quite," said Gordon.

Carol slid back in her chair, gave a satisfied sigh.

"Your first senior adventure," she said. "Bingo night at the *old-folks home*?"

"Senior center," Gordon stated firmly. "Very funny."

"Of course, of course. As you say. Senior center."

The four of them quietly took in the morning, looking out at their neighborhood from their place on Gordon's porch.

"This is nice, Dad," said Carol. "The old neighborhood. Nice."

"That it is," said Gordon.

Coming up the street then, Lloyd, tall wooden staff in hand. A casual, easy pace. He came to a stop as he reached Gordon's. He slowly turned his head, looking up, in the direction of the four sitting on the porch.

He gave a smooth, acknowledging nod, held it a long moment. He looked forward then and started again, his casual, easy pace, up the street.

"Yup," said Gordon then. "This is nice."

~ end...

www.ingramcontent.com/pod-product-compliance
Lightning Source LLC
Chambersburg PA
CBHW022053170626
46808CB00003B/1460